Against

The

Wall

by Julie Prestsater

Credits

Dedication

This one is for all my teacher friends. To ... when the bell rings ... and all the good times that follow.

Chapter One

Love Quarrel Stirs Violence among High School Teachers. I can just picture the headlines if I were to lose control and hit that hussy square in the jaw.

But there she goes looking all superior, and I feel the urge to rip out her dark brown extensions and shove them straight down her throat. As tempting as it may be, I know for the sake of my career, I can't just haul off and knock someone out—and especially not over a guy. What kind of example would I be setting in a hallway full of hormonal adolescent students? So I guess I can understand why dating someone at work is not encouraged, especially when I want to punch that man-stealing whore. If she wasn't such a floozy, maybe I could move on. Maybe I wouldn't want him back so badly if he had left me for someone less sleazy. Not this waif in six-inch stilettos, acrylic nails, smothered in every possible product from the MAC counter. But this is who—or what—he chose. And yes, I still want him so bad it hurts.

A group of chatty kids snap me out of my frenzy.

"Check her out. I'd like to tap that ass," a squirrely freshman boy says, raising eyebrows at the previously mentioned man-stealing whore, my colleague—a science teacher—walking down the hall as if it were an America's Next Top Model runway. If she were in my class, I'd send her out for dress code violations on a daily basis. There's no doubt she heard him too, and liked it. If only I was a student again, I'd be tempted to stick glue in her body lotion during gym. That would wipe the smile off her face.

"I know right, if she were homework, I'd do her every night," his friend replies. They slap hands wildly in agreement. Great. Not only do half the male teachers here want her, the students are even drooling over this hoochie.

"Gross," one of the girls in the huddle says, smacking Boy #2 in the chest.

Another young lady chimes in, "Dude, she's a teacher. That's so wrong."

"So," Boy #1 retorts. "I'm sure teachers like to get it on." He pumps his hips back and forth, reminding me of Peewee from the old Porky's movies. Sucking back the urge to gag, I have to stop myself from going over to them and smacking him in the back of the head. Little pervert.

"Eww. They're so old. That's just nasty on so many levels." Girl #2 shudders at the thought. Now, I want to smack her.

"Yeah, it's like admitting our parents have sex. There's no way teachers do it," Girl #1 adds. Okay, I'm about to do a whole heck of a lot of smacking. These children are going to need ice packs when I'm done with them for all their stupid talk. We're teachers, not nuns and priests. No vow of celibacy here.

"Thanks," he pauses, staring her down. "You totally killed it." Boy #2 stalks off into class. The others follow, snickering.

Brats!

The bell rings. A few stragglers rush through the door just as I'm about to close it, and I have the overwhelming desire to change my welcome back spiel.

Good morning losers! Just a FYI. Teachers do have sex. Just like we eat, shit, and sleep every day. We also have to go to the grocery store so don't be in shock when you see me at Albertson's and I have a box of Tampax in my cart. I also have to buy clothes, so you might also see me at the mall and if you even make a face when I hit the dressing room with a year's supply of Spanx, I may be forced to mark your papers with a big fat bleeding F for the rest of the year. So, yes, teachers have sex! And it's not gross and it's not like your parents doing it either. But for crying out loud, gentlemen, don't go blind fantasizing about that skank you saw in the hall. She doesn't have sex. She just fucks—excuse my language.

Damn it. Listening to student chatter before class has totally thrown me for a loop. I'm totally off my first-day-of-school game. My students are looking up at me like little puppies wanting table food, and I don't have any scraps. I can't think of shit to say.

The ridiculous conversation between a bunch of sex-crazed teenagers should really have little effect on me. I wouldn't be bothered if those skinny little boys were talking about anyone else. But no…, they're poppin' chubs over Ms. McGallian. And, while teachers do have sex, and Ms. McGallian is having plenty, I for one, am not. I'm not even fucking for Christ's sake. Oh shit, I just said Christ and fuck in the same sentence. Scratch that. I just said shit, Christ, and fuck in the same sentence. Twice.

One more thing … we fucking cuss too, bitches.

While I wait for my Lean Cuisine to cool down enough to *not* cause first degree burns in my mouth, I notice my lunch isn't the only thing sizzling. The anger boils in my gut, and I wish it wasn't. I honestly wish I didn't care so much.

"Come on, Shel. It's the first day back and you're already showing your fangs. You look like you wanna rip off her head, shred her to pieces, and burn her hoochified remains," my bestie tells me, hand on her hip in disapproval.

Lowering my head at her, I try my hardest to give her *the look*. "Mel, the Twilight references are getting old. Besides, you're thirty-two. Can you please move beyond YA books and fantasize about guys who are legal?" I ask my best friend of twenty-two years.

"Edward is legal. He's over a hundred years old." Melissa, who I've called Mel since the fourth grade, tosses her lunch on the table and sits next to me. "And I'm married. I dream about every man I see, or read about. Thank God for fantasies or I'd never get the chance to be manhandled by so many beautiful men."

Allowing a grin to form, I have to try to stop full blown laughter so I won't encourage her antics. "Yeah well, you're a slut in your fantasies."

She takes a huge bite of her sandwich and says, with grape jelly oozing out the side of her mouth, "I guess that makes me a fantastic slut." She winks at me and I can't help but laugh. She always manages to make me feel better. "Oh shit, here we go, Shel. Be cool."

"What?" I ask, watching Mel tense up and take a deep breath.

"He's here."

He's here?

And by he, she means my ex-boyfriend. My ex-loveofmylife. My ex-almostthefatherofmychildren. My ex-happilyeverafter. My ex-fiancé. My ex who left me for that Kim Kardashian butt double, Ms. McGallian. He'd argue he didn't leave me for the curvy brunette with the million dollar highlights, big boobs, and scary acrylic nails. Of course he didn't. I mean, they started dating less than a month after he called it quits. Yet, I'm supposed to believe she had nothing to do with it. She's had practically every single man, a few of them married, on this damn campus and she couldn't let my guy escape her claws. No. She dug right in and he didn't even try to run from little Ms. Fake-Everything-From-Head-To-Toe.

I don't see him, but I'm sure he sees Mel's sneer. She's practically stabbing a dagger through his chest with her eyes. Maybe she could will his pecker to fall off. That seems like a fair punishment for dumping my ass after ten plus years.

But, that was last year. Summer vacation should've been enough time for me to lick my wounds and get over the bastard, but one look at him and my heart turns to mush all over again. His thick black hair is getting long and wavy, and I want to go over there and grab a handful of it. He must have gone shopping. I've never seen that shirt before. It actually has bling on it. She probably bought it for him. The Chase I know would never wear a shirt with wings on it. But whatever. The Chase I know would have never dumped the woman he was engaged to either.

"Stop with the eyes already," Mel whispers, kicking me under the table.

"Ow. What the hell?"

She glares down at me, big Betty Boop brown eyes, with unnaturally long lashes, bulging from their sockets. Her eyes are the only thing big about my best friend. She's this petite little thing. Barely five feet tall, having stopped growing in the sixth grade. "Don't even look at him with those sad, pathetic eyes. It's been four months. Don't let him see you like this. Don't let *her*." Too bad her mouth isn't small and gentle like her frame. Her brash sassy talk more than makes up for her elfin size.

Julie Prestsater

I can't help glancing over at their table again. My eyes meet the tramp's and I'm certain I see a smirk on her face. Give me five seconds alone with this bitch. She'll be declawed in three, and with the other two, I'll punch her in each tit just for fun. I know I shouldn't take it all out on her, but Mel has Chase taken care of. Right about now, his balls are being hacked off with an ax in her mind.

Four months is clearly not long enough to get over someone you've been with half your life, I want to tell Mel. But I don't. My shin still stings from her swift kick and rubbing it like crazy is keeping me from looking in the happy couple's direction, again. I must look like an idiot massaging up and down my leg, but it beats the alternative. Repeatedly seeing Ms. McGallian and my ex together will make this first day of school the worst in my career. Although, I'm pretty sure this entire year is going to kill me.

I may need to rethink my profession. Or maybe consider a transfer, at the very least. When people break up and go their separate ways, the dumpee is bound to get over the dumper after days and days apart. There's just one huge problem here: the dumpee and the dumper will be seeing each other five days a week, along with the ho bag who is now shacking up with the dumper. Now, the dumpee is feeling even dumpier.

"I'm gonna start eating in my classroom." It seems impossible to handle another day like this one, where I have to concentrate on not letting my eyes wander.

Mel shoots me another irritated look. "Don't you dare. You are *not* going to let them force you to hide out in your room all year. They should be the ones who hide in shame. But that bitch wants to rub it in your face." She's right. She always is. I shouldn't let her get to me.

"FYI … if I can hear this conversation on the other side of the room, so can they," a voice whispers in my ear. I look up and I'm eye to eye with Matty. He gives me a sympathetic look, squeezes my shoulder, and walks away.

"Dang, that guy wants you so bad," Mel says quietly, fluttering her brows at me.

"Mr. Fuller is a good friend. It's not like that," I remind her.

"Well as I've heard on many Lifetime Movie Originals, 'the best way to get over a man is to get under another one'. I doubt Matt Fuller will mind being on top if you know what I mean."

"You're scandalous."

Get under another one? Is she crazy? I guess if I ever did manage to get *under* another man, Matty would be high on my list of choices, if only we didn't work together. Whose list wouldn't he be on? The man is delicious with his bright blue eyes that twinkle every time he smiles, and his well-built physique and bronze skin. Every inch of his six-foot body is beautiful, inside and out. If I had to choose between him and Chase based solely on looks, Matty would beat him every day of the week. Chase is great looking and uber sexy. Women check Chase out all the time. But Matty, he's absolutely gorgeous and there's not an arrogant cell in his entire body. Now, there's the major difference between the two men.

And one more thing while I'm thinking about over and under, top and bottom.

If and when I decide to 'get over' my sexy, cheating ex, I will most definitely be *on top*.

Weeks later, I'm eating my Trader Joe's Pasadena Salad in my classroom. Alone. Mel refuses to eat with me. She's so damn stubborn. I know she wants too, but she keeps telling me, "It's the principality."

Principality—that's not even a word. Not in the way she's using it. And she's an English teacher. Go figure.

The door opens slowly as I stuff my mouth with a forkful of lettuce, almonds, and chicken. I almost choke when I see who it is. In fact, I knew who it was the moment I caught a whiff of the air wafting in with him. Chase has been wearing Eternity for Men since we were in high school. I'm surprised Ms. Blingyshirts hasn't changed his scent too. At any rate, his timing couldn't be worse. My mouth is overflowing and I can barely chew. Time plays in slow motion as he makes his way to my desk. How anyone can look so sexy just merely walking is beyond me. There are no words to describe it. I blink hard and fast to snap myself out of his trance. Spitting back a wad of half-chewed salad in its container, I sneer, "What the hell do you want?"

Like my strategy? In an effort to not break down and cry hysterically every time I'm alone with this asshole, I have to be mean. I can't bring myself to be civil because every time I do, I end up asking him what went wrong and how I can fix it. As if I'm the one who needs fixing. Okay, maybe the fact that my innards are blubbering fools right now is evidence of that, but I can't let him get to me. So instead, I just act like a bitch. It's the only way to survive this stupid ass break-up.

I'm snarling at him, yet he smiles.

If my heels weren't digging in the floor, I'd slide off my seat leaving snail trails behind. This man can make me ache down there with just an effing smile. It's a wonder how he can still do that with our long history together. For most people, doesn't that sort of thing fizzle out after a few years?

He doesn't say anything right away, so I utter again, "Well. What is it?"

He ignores my question and says as nonchalant as can be, "Hey, hon, how you been?"

Hon? Really? Un-frickin'-believable.

Raising my right brow, I give him the most disapproving look I can muster. "Just great, *Dear*," I sneer with a snap of my neck.

"I haven't seen you during lunch in a while," his voice softens.

"It's too crowded in the staff lounge." Translation: I don't want to see you and your nasty ass girlfriend.

"Aw, come on. You should come down." Translation: making you feel like shit is so much more fun in public.

"I've got a lot of grading to do." Looking down at my desk, I notice just one small stack of papers. Shit.

That's what I get for having nothing better to do than grade papers night after night.

He sits on my nearly empty desk. "Well, I hear everybody misses you." He plumps out his bottom lip in a pout. I think my heart just stopped. Is he trying to kill me? Could he be prosecuted for murder? Cause of death: broken heart. Murder weapon: words laced with bullshit. It's me who should be thrown in jail for eating up every one of those words. But, I can't help myself.

Okay, Shel, relax. Keep it cool. Back to bitch mode.

I summon the courage to shout at him, "Shut the hell up and get the fuck out of my room. And don't come back unless it's about work. Even then, don't bother. Just send me an email."

"Shel Belle, don't be that way. I still wanna be friends." Oh no he didn't just pull out the friend card. He needs to shove that crap back from wherever he yanked it from. He's so full of shit, no wonder his skin is so tan.

"Friends, my ass. We've been friends since the second grade, since I kissed you on the cheek on Space Mountain when you were so scared you wanted to cry. I should have just let you piss your pants and never talked to you again and I wouldn't be in this mess." I glare at him with as much pissiness as I can exude. "Fuck friends. I have enough friends. I don't need any more. And I sure as hell don't need you. So get to steppin', Chase." Tears threaten to bubble over the edge of my eyelids but I will them back. I swear to God, if I cry in his presence, I'll kick my own ass.

Chase's chocolate brown eyes glare at me, his nose flares, and I can see the muscles in his jaw twitch, but I don't say another word and my tears don't fall. But his do. He gets up and walks out my door. Before it slams, my heart fails me and tears start streaming down my heated face like a flash flood.

He has no right getting teary-eyed on me. He did this. I didn't break up with him. He can't toss me aside, put me in the junk drawer and come find me when he needs me.

I can't still be his friend. It doesn't work like that. How can we possibly be buddies? Am I supposed to chat with him about the good old days, or go out to dinner with him and what's her face? I don't know how we can go from long-term relationship to friends with everything just peachy. That's bullshit.

The bell rings. Son of a mother lover. I grab for the box of tissues near my computer and blot my already puffy eyes. There's no way I can camouflage this. I just hope my class doesn't say anything. I'll probably cry more.

"Ms. Gelson, are you okay?" Meg, my student aide, asks.

Trying to muffle my sniffling noises, I force myself to respond. "Oh, I'm fine honey. Nothing some chocolate and a little makeup can't fix." I open the bottom drawer to my desk to reveal a rather large bag of Dove dark chocolates. Too bad I can't rig a keg of beer in my desk. Or maybe squeeze a twelve pack in my mini-fridge. I wish. For some reason, I don't think chocolate is going to cure this one.

"I saw Mr. Marino leaving and he looked like crap. Don't worry. It's not gonna last, ya know. My best friend, Keesha, is his aide this year and she says she's rallying for you. She wants him to dump that big assed beeyotch soon. She's so fake with her caked on makeup and hooker heels. She reminds me of my ex-best friend. You have class, something Ms. McG doesn't. Marino will figure it out." I look at her all wide-eyed, and she says, "Oh, sorry. I shouldn't have said that. I forget you're my teacher."

I can remember comforting her when she was a freshman and found out her best friend was doing the deed with her boyfriend. Can you imagine having to deal with that level of drama when you're fourteen? I wish I could tell her it gets better. But what I want to do is hug her, and say thank you. I knew there was a reason I liked her. I should buy her lunch.

My students fill their desks and immediately get started on the bell-ringer—the assignment I posted on the board. I sense the whispers, but I don't look up. I take attendance, all the while thinking about Chase. I wonder if Ms. McGallian knows about his little lunchtime visit. I doubt *she's* included in the masses of people who miss me at lunch. If she doesn't know he stopped by, she will by the end of the period. If there's anything I know about my school and my students, it's information spreads like the plague. Right now, Meg is on her cell texting, and I'd bet a hundred bucks she's telling her friends. I wish I could see Ms. Fiancé-Stealer's face when she finds out her man left my room all weepy.

Let the games begin, bitches!

Chapter Two

Mel and I are part of a handful of people who arrive at our staff meetings early. Like bad students, we sit in the back of the room where we have a clear view of everyone as they walk in. This comes to our advantage when the bobbles—our bosses who mumble and nod away like bobble heads—start doing their thing, chattering away even though less than half the staff is actually listening. Mel's a natural born shit talker and this is an optimal environment for endless sources of material.

We're definitely not the only ones being rude though. Teachers truly make the worst audience. Talking, texting, cracking jokes. All behaviors I'd never accept from my own students, yet I break the same rules during these meetings. It's not like there are any consequences though. As if the dean is going to come by and confiscate my phone. I might just die laughing if she ever did.

"Ooo. Look at him," Mel says, sitting at the edge of her seat. "I think he's the new history teacher. His ass looks nice in those fitted slacks. Mm... I just wanna bite it," she clacks her teeth together and growls.

"No way. I'm not gonna hook up with anyone from work. I already told you. It's bad enough having one ex here. I don't need a collection of them." I take a swig of my 7-Eleven coffee. "He's probably gay though. His pants are way too tight. Or maybe, metrosexual. Do people still say that?" He is hot though. Very clean-cut and well dressed. He probably has a standing appointment with his barber to get his hair trimmed every week to keep crisp lines like those. I wouldn't doubt he uses expensive gel too, and has more beauty products than me. Yes, I assume all this from the high quality of pressed creases in his dress pants, and the flawless hairline around a perfectly messy faux hawk.

"I haven't heard that term in a while. Metrosexual is just closet gay anyway." Mel bites into her bagel, and says through a mouthful of dough, "What about him? He is one fine specimen."

I look where she gestured in the front row. Uh-huh. He is fine. How did we get so lucky to be surrounded by good looking men? If things hadn't gone so terribly wrong with Chase, I'm thinking this would be a promising profession to be in to land a hot guy.

But this one is taken. "He's married," I remind her.

"So. As if it matters to anyone else at work." True. With all the hook-ups, set-ups, and infidelity on campus, the stories these walls could tell would make for fascinating reality TV. The Real Teachers of Carver High. Can you imagine? That would be stinking awesome. I'd actually watch reality TV for once. A bunch of teachers sitting around throwing back glasses of beer and wine, talking crap about their students who pissed them off today, or about what Johnny's mom was wearing to the parent conference. Haha. It would be a blast.

"Well it matters to me," I tell her. "I'm no homewrecker."

"Maybe I'll jump on him."

"You're not jumping on anyone."

"I know," she says through another mouthful of bagel, cream cheese smeared across part of her lip.

"Hey, ladies," Matty says. "Thanks for saving me a seat." He squeezes by Mel, and then plops himself next to me. His knees almost hit the chair in front of us. These rows aren't far enough apart for people his size. I'm sure he always has this problem. Me? Not so much. Sometimes my feet don't reach the floor at the movies, depending on what theater we go to. I never have to worry about my knees hitting the seat in front of me.

"Of course we did," Mel says, winking at me. I dig my elbow in her side.

I don't say anything, but his scent makes me smile. Very earthy, like he just took a shower in the woods using man soap. I love that smell. If I wasn't a girl, I'd use it myself.

"Hey Matt, did you bring lunch today?" Mel asks him, breaking the silence.

"Nah, gotta hit the snack bar. Why?"

"Perfect," she squeals. "Shels brought me lunch today, but I brought leftovers and I have a parent conference anyway so I don't want the food to go to waste. Why don't you have lunch with her? Just go to her room right when the bell rings, okay?" Wow. She said that all in one breath. Does she need an oxygen mask now?

Matty nudges me in the arm. "Does that work for you, Shel?"

Well, what am I going to say? No. Don't come. I don't want to share with you. Of course it's fine. He's my friend and it's been a long time since we've had a good chat. "Duh. It's nothing big though. Don't expect a gourmet meal or anything," I murmur trying to make light of our pending meal.

"I've been eating your cookin' for five years. I know better than to expect gourmet." He brushes his shoulder against mine, and I slap his knee.

Mel pushes my elbow off the arm rest and I glance her way. She winks again and I read her lips, *Foreplay*. Rolling my eyes at her, I face forward and fake paying attention to the meeting.

My cell buzzes and I glance at the text.

Keep it up and ull b touchng his 3rd leg soon ;)

Trying to shield my phone, I feel like the words are flashing like a neon sign over my head. I seriously hope Matty can't see my screen. Thinking about her remark, I laugh inside. She's too funny.

Guess we're done trying to find my next bf in the crowd, I text her back.

Don't need 2. He's sittin rite next 2 u.

Going out with Matty would be so easy. Perfect actually. Until I get sick of him or he gets sick of me and then we're doomed. I'll be right back where I started but without one of my closest friends. Sure, I know he likes me. Maybe. It's probably one of those things when you like someone just because you can't have them, and when you finally get them, it sucks. The novelty wears off and neither person can run away fast enough. I don't want that to happen. Matty means way too much to me to take the risk. I'd rather he be a friend forever than a quick roll in the hay for however long I can keep him interested.

Stealing a glance at him, I notice he didn't shave this morning. The golden brown stubble against his bronze skin catches the artificial lighting in here and it's like it's saying hello to me. Like, *Hey I wanna rub this five o'clock shadow all over you.* Wow. A twinge hits me between my thighs. Damn, where did those prickles darting all over my body come from? It's like *that* with just a glimpse of facial hair. It's a good thing I didn't gaze into his gorgeous eyes. Crystal blue, and I'm talking "ocean in Hawaii you can see right through to the sand", blue. He has the kind of eyes that speak to you. Just one look at them and you can always tell what kind of mood he's in, which is usually a good one. This man is perpetually happy. Always smiling, showing the little creases around the corners of his eyes.

"Shels," a voice is calling me. "Shelly. Hello," Matty says, putting his hand on top of mine. My girl parts contract with the touch of his warm palm on the back of my hand. "We still good for lunch?"

I shake my head clear and realize everyone is getting up to leave. "Uh. Yeah. Sure."

"You want me to get us some drinks?" His baby blues question me.

I glance down and his hand remains resting on mine. He notices too, and pulls away quickly like he touched something that burned his skin. "No, that's okay. I have some."

He stands up and gestures to me to do the same. Mel is already waiting by the door. As we reach her, Matty puts his hand on my lower back and I gaze up at him. "I'll see you at lunch," he says, and I can't keep my eyes off his mouth. It's like I hear the words as his lips move in slowmo. He grins at me, one corner of his mouth turning upward. My legs quiver as he walks away, and begins talking to another teacher. Uh oh. I think I'm in trouble.

Mel is watching me with a ridiculously giddy smile spread across her face.

"It's happening," she sings.

"I hate you," I tell her, and we walk to our classrooms in silence.

The first four periods leading up to lunch seem like eons passing. Mountain ranges and miles of new ocean floor were probably created in the same amount of time it took for the lunch bell to ring. The *Grapes of*

Wrath could've been written during these hours of maddening impatience. I've literally popped two tins of Altoids trying to make sure my breath is fresh for my lunch time rendezvous. I know I'm making more out of this than it is. It's just a casual lunch between two friends who just happen to work together. Nothing is happening. Matty isn't interested in me like that. Well, maybe he is but he'd never act on it. He knows I'm damaged goods, and not completely over Chase. And how many times have I said I don't want to date anyone at work? How many? Like five thousand. So why am I freaking out over lunch? Relax, Shel. It's going to be just fine. Just breathe.

I inhale and exhale a large gasp of air just as Matty walks in the door. Thankfully, all my last minute stragglers have packed up their stuff and gone before he arrives. I can just picture the rumors spreading all over school. Ms. Gelson and Mr. Fuller were all hugged up during lunch. And that's just the start of it. By the end of the day, I'd most likely be pregnant with twins and have some sort of fictitious sexually transmitted disease.

But he's here now, and we're alone. No need to worry about the buzz just yet.

As he steps toward me, smiling, I absorb his presence. His characteristic Levi jeans sit low on his waist, and if he were to turn around and model for me, I could stare at his perfectly round ass filling out his pants. A short-sleeved button-up shirt hugs his shoulders just enough to show off his muscles but not so much that he looks like he's wearing his little brother's clothes. I don't know what brand it is, but it's stylish. He looks quite appetizing.

It strikes me as odd that I'm checking him out in such a way. Why am I noticing these things about him now? In a way that makes my stomach flip-flop and my heart race. Just like I thought it was weird when I took note of his scent earlier. He's always looked this good. He's not doing anything different. So why now do I want to tear off his clothes and have my way with him on my desk?

"Hey, I brought dessert." He holds up two Rice Krispies Treats from the student store.

I smile my big smile, hoping he can't tell I was just violating him in my thoughts. "Yummy. Maybe we should do dessert first." And I'm not talking about the Rice Krispies either. *Oh, girl, you need to stop*, I tell myself.

"You got quite the spread going on here." Chicken fajitas, rice, beans, fresh guacamole, salsa, chips, and tortillas. If this was a date, I'm pretty sure

Matty would want to marry me after this feast. "Where did you pick this up?" Okay, so he knows me too well to believe I cooked all this.

"You suck! Don't believe I cooked, huh?" I tease him.

He takes a plate and starts making himself some tacos. "Not a chance." He chuckles.

"Okay, you got me. That new Mexican restaurant by the mall. Good stuff. Dig in."

We make small talk in between bites of deliciousness.

We reminisce about a conference we had to go to last year in Minnesota of all places. In the state of a million lakes, we couldn't find anything to do but go to the Mall of America every day. He convinced me to go on all the rides at the amusement park in the center of the mall. Mel refused to join in, instead she took pictures of us on each ride making wacky faces, most of which looked like I was ready to barf.

I glance at him and smile. He looks at me and smiles.

Feels like the best twenty minutes of my life.

"The bell's about to ring," he says, standing and beginning to clear our plates.

"Don't worry about it. I'll get it. My kids are working on a quiz as soon as the bell rings. You should get going."

"Well, thank you, Shel. " He steps toward me. "Next time, it's on me. But dinner." I look up at him, trying not to study his mouth but I can't help it. He licks his lips and the moisture left behind makes me want to lap it up with my tongue. He bends down getting closer, and the scent of his subtle cologne, combined with the spices of our meal, fills my senses and I'm whirling. Matty gently kisses my left cheek and his lips linger for a split second while he squeezes my hand. "Think of me when you have your dessert," he says as he turns away and walks out of my classroom, leaving me stunned and speechless.

After school when I finally have time to relax and enjoy my marshmallow treat. Leaning back in my chair, I put my feet up on my desk and tear open the blue foil wrapper. Instantly, I can feel Matty's lips on my cheek along with his warm breath. *Think of me*, he had said. It worked. I'm thinking of him all right. I feel like his scent has lingered in my room and if I could just bottle it up and take it home with me, I'd have some night. Smiling, I take a small nibble out of the corner of my dessert imagining what it would be like to sprinkle his throat with gentle pecks from my lips. The taste is sweet in my mouth and my girl parts tighten. Another small bite and as I chew I think about kissing his chest. Matty's always looked amazing without a shirt on, bare chiseled chest, until you reach the little happy trail leading down into the place I've never been before, but suddenly want to be. Even though I was with Chase, I never wasted an opportunity to check Matty out at any pool parties for work. I find myself licking my fingers at the thought. If only he knew what he could do to me without even being in the room.

"Must be some Rice Krispies Treat. Are you sure there isn't something other than marshmallow whip in there?" Bobbling the treat in my hands, I nearly fall out of my seat, whipping my feet off my desk and trying to sit up. "I've never wanted to be a piece of puffed rice so much before in my whole life."

"Oh shit, Chase. Why the hell do you say crap like that?" Chomping on the last piece, I chew like a dog, irritated he ruined my moment of bliss.

"Because I mean it, Shel Belle. In all our years together, I don't think you ever looked like that when you thought about me." He walks over and stands in front of me, so I'm eye level with his zipper and my dear old friend who I haven't seen in quite some time. The idea is enough to make me forget about Matty, and images of Chase's ass in my hands as I bring him into my mouth take hold of me.

Chase runs his hand through my hair and clutches the back of my neck. I stare up into his mocha eyes and they call to me. He misses me. He really does. My throat goes dry, but I have to say something. I can't just sit here with his hand wrapped up in my hair and my mind inside his pants. "Chase, what are you doing here?" I whimper. I consider his flirtatious words again and my heart skips.

"I need you, Shel Belle. I screwed up. I want you back."

How long have I waited to hear those words?

Standing up to wrap my arms around his waist, I allow myself to rest my head in the place where it fits perfectly just below his chin. He drapes his arms around me and holds me tight. I feel like the wind has been knocked out of me and I tell myself to breathe. Slowly, I inhale through my nose and try to soak up everything that's happening so I'll never forget it.

Something's off though. His touch feels the same. His body feels the same in my arms. We still mesh together like two parts of a whole. Even with all these things that seem so familiar, something is definitely wrong.

I tilt my head up and he bends down to nuzzle my neck. I brush my nose against his cool skin and inhale the man who has been mine for years. And that's when I figure it out. His cologne. It's different. It's still the same sweet smell of Eternity, but mixed with another odor. A hint of jasmine. The scent I have pressed against my lips right now isn't Chase's. It's her perfume. Or maybe her it's her body lotion, her shampoo, or body wash. A fragrance I never want to smell again. Not while the man I still love is telling me he wants me back.

I muster up all the strength I have to push him away so I can look into his eyes for answers, for the truth.

"Chase?"

He looks down at me, rests his arms on my shoulders, and kisses the top of my head. I wish I could just let this go and enjoy the moment, but I can't.

"Chase?" I mutter.

"Yeah, hon. What is it?"

My throat tightens, but I ask anyway. "What about Summer?" Saying Ms. McGallian's first name makes her more than just a teacher I see in the halls on a daily basis. More than just the person I've seen snickering at me during lunch. Saying her name makes her a real woman. The woman who Chase left me for.

"What about her?" His body goes rigid.

"Well, you said you wanted me back. It has to mean you guys aren't together anymore, right?" The guilty expression in his eyes breaks what's left of my bleeding heart all over again. I'm such a fucking idiot.

"Well ... " he hovers on the word. Instantly, I back away from him.

"Well, what, Chase?" I want to kick my ass for asking. Why can't I summon my bitch façade right now? My evil twin.

"I can't break up with Summer, Shel. "

"Well then explain to me how we can get back together." I snarl at him. I need duct tape. A gag. Something to keep me from making myself sound even more pitiful. Why do I let him do this?

He raises his hands and rubs them up and down my arms. "Well, I was just thinking maybe ... "

I see the conniving look in his eyes and I know exactly what he is thinking.

Okay, I may as well turn green and tear off my clothes. This bitch is back. I'm not taking anymore shit from this fucker.

"Maybe what? That we can just hook up and *I* can be the other woman this time."

"Well, yeah. I mean, no. I don't know. I just came in here to see how your lunch date went. It's all over school you and Fuller are fucking. And then I saw you violating that Rice Krispie and I swear, I got hard just watching you. I need you. He needs you," he says, pulling me into his erection.

He needs me? I don't know what the hell for. If he enjoyed having sex with me as much as I did with him, wouldn't we still be together? He makes my cooch hotter with just the anticipation of sex more than the act itself. Never again will I allow this poor excuse for a man to make me twitch down there. So fuck what *he needs*.

Fighting the urge to knee him in the balls, I back away from him once more. He has to be kidding me. Glaring at him, I search for the words to tell him he's a bastard and I never want to see him again. He's a total ass and I can't believe I stayed with him as long as I did. I should be grateful he finally showed his true colors and ditched me before the wedding. Yet, I still don't feel so lucky.

This jackass just continues to break my heart over and over again. Just when I think I can move on, he sweeps in and screws that up too.

I take a deep breath, look straight into his eyes, and dig my pointer finger into his chest.

"Chase, I need you to understand something. You need to walk out that door and not come back in here or I'll file a grievance against you for sexual harassment. Get the fuck out and ... Leave. Me. The. Hell. Alone."

"Shel Belle," he mutters, taking my hand from his chest.

"I mean it, Chase," I shout, trembling from head to toe.

"But ... " he begins to protest for a second time.

"She said, 'get out'," Matty's voice booms. I'm happy for anyone to save me from this mess, or from myself. But not Matty. Instantly, I wonder how long he's been standing there. I wonder how much he's seen or heard.

Chase whips around. His face hardens when he sees Matty. "Fuller, this has nothing to do with you." He takes a step forward, almost pushing me aside.

Matty slowly walks toward us. "Uh, maybe not, but if Shelly wants you gone, you better get out before I call security."

Chase lets out a chuckle. "You fucking pansy. Can't handle me yourself, so you have to call for back up," he says, closing the gap between the two of them.

Oh shit.

"I can handle you just fine but we're at work, and I'm trying my hardest to be professional," Matty responds.

Rushing to jump between them before they hit chests, I plant my feet in front of Chase and plead with him, "Just go, Chase. Just go." For the first time, I notice their difference in height. Matty is much taller than Chase, and outweighs him as well. Matty is muscular, Chase is fit but not chiseled.

"You've been sniffing around her ass for I don't know how long, Fuller. Shel's finally single and you just couldn't wait to start screwing her, huh? It won't last though. She still loves me. She always will. But if you don't mind tasting me every time you're with her, be my guest." Matty lunges at him and Chase quickly steps around me and out of his way. "Now now, Mr. Fuller, don't forget to be professional," he says before leaving the room. I should have let Matty pummel him.

"Holy shit! That son of a bitch," I yell.

Matty takes me in his arms and runs his hands up and down my back. "Shh … There are kids still out there."

"When in the hell did Chase turn into such an asshole?" I ask. It's like he has multiple personalities or something. When he came in, he was totally smooth and flirty, but then he morphed into a total dickhead. I can't believe he just said that too. He can't possibly think Matty and I are sleeping together. The rumor mill must be on heightened alert or something, and obviously, totally inaccurate.

Matty chuckles. "He's always been an asshole."

I step back from him. "Really? He was always great, until Summer came along."

"Love is blind," he says, chuckling again.

"I guess," I tell him. Trying to make light of things, I add, "Hey, so according to C-High's very own gossip channel, I hear we're fucking each other's brains out."

"Cool. Are you enjoying it as much as I am?" he jokes.

"Oh, so much more," I tease. "You'd think people would have something better to do than make shit up."

"Yeah, but this is high school. A juicy piece of dirt is so much better than the truth."

I consider this. "Yeah, I guess super hot sex with a good looking guy is better than watching Lifetime movies alone in your sweats." Did I just admit I watch movies in sweats all night? Aloud? I must look like a sad excuse for a woman.

"So you think I'm good looking?" His eyes crinkle in the corners. Very cute.

"Oh. Sure. Of course you are. But I was just making a generalization. Not necessarily talking about us and hot sex or something." Boy, it's getting hot in here, and the air conditioning is running full blast in my classroom.

"Well Chase did mention us screwing, but I like the way you make it sound so much better." He flashes his sexy smile at me and his blue eyes pierce through me like a spark of electricity.

"Alrighty then," I say, fanning myself.

"Am I making you blush?" he asks, running his fingers through his hair.

"Probably," I concede. "Anyway, I'm sorry you had to deal with Chase." Looking at the floor trying to avoid eye contact, I feel the need to move the conversation past the sexy talk.

"No worries, Shel. I'm glad I showed up when I did. I was just coming by to see if you wanted to have dessert together." He holds up his little blue package.

"Ah... I was enjoying it when the bastard came in. Sorry."

"I can share this one with you." Earlier, I would have taken him up on the offer. It wasn't long ago when I was practically having a wet dream at my desk at the thought of Matty. And it also wasn't long ago that I was looking up into Chase's eyes from zipper level before he so rudely asked me to be his sidedish fuck buddy.

I pat Matty on the arm and tell him, "You go ahead and have that one for yourself. I have to get going." I turn to go back to my desk, but Matty catches my hand to stop me.

"Shel, don't let him ruin this. We had a great time today at lunch, right?" He looks at me for reassurance.

"Right, I really enjoyed it. It's probably the most fun I've had in a long time," I admit. He deserves to know the truth. I can't bull shit him.

"I have no doubt you would still be thinking about it if Chase hadn't come in here, which I'm sure he did only because he heard about us and was jealous."

"You're probably right. But ... " I pause, trying to find the words. I want to be honest, but I don't want to be heartless either. "I still have feelings for him, Matty. You made me forget all about him today, and then he came in here and took it all away. He said he wanted me back and I was ready to jump at the chance. You don't deserve to be treated that way."

"And neither do you," he tells me. "He's going to keep coming back and playing with your mind, as long as you let him. He doesn't want to see you happy with anyone else, yet he won't commit to you either. If he just let you go, you could move on and be happy."

With my head down, I kick around some dirt on the floor and chew on my bottom lip. I know he's right.

"You can either wait around for him to let you go, or you can move on without his help. It's up to you. It's your life you're letting someone else control," he says with a shrug.

I really don't know what to say. He totally has me pegged.

The silence must get to him because he shakes his head, and says, "I'm sorry. I probably shouldn't have said anything. I'll talk to you later."

Within seconds, Matty is gone too. And within minutes, I wish he wasn't.

"This is exactly why I don't want to date anyone from work," I yell into the phone at Mel.

I hear her dogs barking in the background. She probably just got home and they're attacking her for attention. "Shel, I'm sorry. Why don't you come over? Nick is working late again."

"Sounds good, I'll be there in a few." I pause to check my rearview mirror, so I don't run over any kids. "Hey, do you have beer?"

"Of course."

Chapter Three

"Talk or beer first?" Mel asks as I walk into her house without knocking. I stopped dealing with those formalities in junior high, when we practically started living at each other's houses. Not much has changed since then. She's married now, but we still have plenty of bestie time.

"Beer!" As if there was any doubt.

"That bad, huh?"

"Yes, that bad." Thinking about Matty, I change my mind. "Well, part of it was good. But still, give me a frickin' beer."

I watch as Mel pours me a Hefeweizen—my drink of choice at home—into a chilled pint-sized glass. She slices up some oranges and squeezes a few into my drink before dropping them in. We should've been bartenders. Making drinks for people while listening to their problems sounds so much more appealing than having issues of my own.

I guzzle half the beer before putting it down. "Yum. That hit the spot." I wipe my mouth with the back of my hand and settle in at her dining room table.

"I should hope so. If you're gonna drink like it's Quarter Beers' Night, we should hit the store before we get too shitty and can't drive." Not a bad idea.

"How many do you have?"

"Twelve pack."

"Should be good. If I still wanna drink, I can move on to that bitch ass wine of yours." I hold out my beer to clink glasses with her rather large goblet of sparkling red bubbly. It may as well be a vase.

"Hey, where are the pooches?" I ask her, looking around the kitchen. They're never too far away from their mama.

"They're resting in my room. I just bought them a new bed and they love it," she explains.

I nod, peeling the wrapper of my beer. "So what's up with Nick? He should pitch a tent and live at the office."

"Don't remind me," she sighs. "If I didn't have you, I'd be alone all the time. I may as well be single." How many times have I heard that? But I guess it's the price you pay for marrying such a successful attorney. I know if I were her, I would be sitting at home all day eating Oreos, reading books, and watching reruns of old soap operas instead of teaching a bunch of high schoolers how to write a complete sentence that actually makes sense. Don't get me wrong, we love our students and our jobs. It's just sometimes they can suck the life right out of you. But then again, one small victory, like a simple thank you or a smile that lights up the face of a struggling reader when he finally gets a C on a test, makes all the hard times worth it.

"Oh stop," I tell her. "I envy you. You have a great husband who takes care of you. You only work because you love it, not because you have to. So he's not home all the time," I pause to take a drink. "At least you don't have him here all day nagging you about cleaning the house, or washing dishes. You get to have a drink with me, and when he gets home, if you feel like it, you can let him manhandle you."

"Yeah, well I guess there are some perks." She gulps down the last of her wine and pours more, while I hit the fridge for another beer. "So tell me what happened that's so bad you're getting liquored up and crashing on my sofa tonight."

"Hmm, where should I start?" I tell her, squeezing some more orange juice in my beer.

"Tell me about lunch. I know it was good because you were giddy as all hell when I talked to you during fifth period."

I look up and watch the blades of the ceiling fan as I revisit my happy time with Matty. We both laughed hysterically when we talked about shopping for prom two years ago. Mel and I dragged him to the mall with us to find dresses to wear as chaperones. We tried on the sluttiest dresses we could find while Matty sat on a sofa in the middle of the store eating popcorn like he was watching Monday Night Football. He's always been chill enough to hang out and have fun with the girls.

In those moments with him, I was so at ease and having such a good time.

I wish I had locked my doors at the end of the day so it wouldn't have been tainted by Chase and his stupid ass remarks.

But, back to my lunch.

"I was giddy, wasn't I?" I smile. "But I ruined it, Mel. I think I hurt him. See. That's why I told you I shouldn't go out with him."

She shakes her head at me. "Shels, it was just lunch for crying out loud. You aren't getting married. Just tell me what happened already."

I try to focus on the good stuff. Matty looked so cute today, and he smelled so damned good. "Okay, so he showed up right after the bell rang. He was adorable. He brought me a Rice frickin' Krispies Treat for dessert."

Mel turns her head to the side, and bats her lashes at me. "Wow," she admonishes. "He's in it big time. He's never shared his cherished treats with me before."

"I know, that's what I was thinking. It was like a declaration or something." Matty loves his Rice Krispies Treats. It's like they are military rations and the only thing standing between him and his last breath. He never shares. In fact, I think he swatted my hand one time when I tried to take one. It's always been a joke between us. I don't touch his treats, and he doesn't touch my beer.

"I know. Totally sweet, huh. We just talked while we ate and we couldn't stop smiling at each other. It was perfect. And then, just before lunch was over he got up to leave."

"Uh-huh. And?" Mel flutters her brows at me.

"He kissed me on the cheek. And he told me to think of him when I ate my dessert."

"And how was it? The kiss?"

I take a quick pull of my beer. "It was on the cheek, Mel." But I know what she means. I felt it. Even though his full lips barely grazed the side of my face, it couldn't have been any better. She glares at me. "Okay, it was amazing, like a damn romance novel. He kind of just lingered there," I touch my cheek. "He barely made contact. Enough for me to be aware his lips were touching me, but not so much he was pouncing on me. It was frickin' picture perfect." Putting my hand to my face again, I wish I could summon that moment back and just bathe in the feeling of it again.

"Oh, if only I could've been there. I feel like I need a box of Ding Dongs and a box of tissues just listening to this."

Instead, she drinks some more wine, and I drink more beer.

"You're silly. Melly Belly!"

"Oh shizzy. Only two beers down and you're already busting out the Melly Bellys."

"Shizzy, Mel? Just two Cougar Town-sized glasses of wine and you're talking like a rapper."

"Fo shizzle, my nizzle g-money. Don't hate the playa, hate the game. You know I'm the *ish*, yo," She crosses her arms in full gangster pose. We both laugh until Mel starts snorting.

"Oh girl, you crazy!" We can't stop laughing. Mel staggers to the fridge to fetch me another beer, and I fill her glass, yet again.

"We need to get new jobs. Listen to us."

I chuckle. "I know. Gangsta rap lingo. Occupational hazard, I suppose."

"You're killing me, Shel. We keep getting off subject. So what happened? How did everything go to shit in a matter of minutes?"

"Oh." Sighing, I force myself back to reality. "My amazing lunch got shit all over when Chase came to see me after school."

"Aha. He couldn't stay away when he heard you were moving on." Mel nods her head as if she's all knowing.

"Something like that I guess. I don't even know how he heard anything. And it's not like Matty and I haven't had lunch together before. Even when Chase and I were together, we would meet for lunch. Why would he think this was any different?" Mel hangs her head low in an admission of guilt. "What did you do?"

"Uh ... I may have mentioned it to one of the girls in the copy room, when I knew he was listening." My mouth drops.

"C'mon, Mel, you know how everyone is. By the time he got to my room, he had it in his mind Matty and I are sleeping together."

"Good," she says. "Let him chew on that for awhile. It's not like he's the only one who can get a piece of ass."

I laugh inside at the thought. I can't remember the last time I got any action. When I do, it's going to be scary. Cobwebs and dust bunnies are probably growing down there.

"Well, you shouldn't have tried to set him off," I scold her.

"I couldn't help it, Shel. He walks around all smug without a care in the world. I wanted him to know you moved on and didn't need him anymore."

"Well, that kinda backfired. He came to see me and then looked at me with those damn Hershey Kiss eyes of his and I melted like an ice cube in the desert. I'm so weak. He said he wanted me back, and I got all weepy thinking it might be true. So I asked him about Summer and that shithead had the nerve to basically say he just wanted me as a little side action, and he wasn't going to break up with her."

"What a cocksucker! You should have just grabbed him by his balls and twisted them all up," she says, with a slur of her words and a fistful of air.

"I wish I would have. I told him to get the fuck out and he wouldn't leave. That's when Matty came in."

Taking a moment for a swig of beer, I notice Mel's big eyes bulging from her head. "Yes, it only gets worse from here."

"Oh shit," Mel's voice gets higher and she rubs her hands together.

"Calm down, sister," I tell her. "Matty told him to leave too. Then they got all *my dick is bigger than your dick*. They puffed out their chests at each other. Chase said some shitty things and left, barely dodging Matty who was about to give him a left hook."

Mel gets us round four. "What did Chase say?" Giving her the run-down of Chase's nasty words and how Matty took off, Mel's face is red with anger. "That rat bastard. I hope he gets diarrhea. Stinky ass bubble guts that make Summer want to puke. I hope they both get the squirts."

A new whirl of laughter ensues as we picture Chase and Summer dealing with bouts of explosive shit.

"Poor Matty. He just left, huh? He'll be okay. That guy likes you so much, he won't let Chase get to him," Mel tries to reassure me. I wish I could believe it. I grab another beer, a bottle of wine, and we head into the family room.

"I don't know," I begin. "I don't really think I should pursue anything with Matty. I know he gets what's going on with Chase, but I can't just lead him on, hoping my feelings for my ex will go away. It's not right. Plus, I can't very well have grown men about to go to blows in my classroom again. I'm not about to get fired over a fling with another staff member."

She punches me on the arm before plopping herself down on the couch. "Stop being such a puss. I don't think it'll come to that. Just keep your bitch up when it comes to Chase, and forget about him. You can't let him string you along forever."

Where have I heard this before? "Did you to talk to Matty? Is there a script for this pep talk? He basically said the same thing earlier."

She chuckles. "Perfect. Matt and I are alike. You can't screw me cause we don't swing like that, but you can do him. What's better than dating your best friend? It's perfect." She is so serious, it's scary. I love her reasoning.

"Yeah, well … until Matty and I are no longer working at the same place of employment, it's not gonna work. I'm putting my foot down. If I'm gonna get some anytime soon, I'm gonna have to extend the search off campus."

"All right, boss," Mel says, holding up her glass to me. "I'll send out the search party soon. We need to get you some action before your va-jay-jay gets moldy." Nice. I think I like cobwebs better.

I put my beer down and take a look at Mel's extensive library of DVDs.

"What should we watch? Should we ogle over the bad boys of Entourage, or drool over McDreamy and McSteamy in Grey's?" I hold up boxed sets of various seasons of each show.

"Ooo. Tough choice. Do I have any Grey's with Avery? He's McScorching hot. Have you seen those eyes?"

Yes, I have. "They remind me of Matty's."

"Ah shit, Shel, I'm sorry. But c'mon, if he has eyes like Avery's how can you not hook up with him? You owe it to yourself and Grey's fans all over the world to start a relationship with a man based on his stunning blue eyes."

She kills me with her crazy talk. "You're a dumb ass. Let's just watch Entourage. One look at Adrian Grenier and all my man troubles will be behind me."

"One look at him, my legs'll be twitching, and I'll be all primed and ready to go when Nick comes home."

"Aw damn. Remind me to put some ear plugs in." I toss a pillow at her head and then we both settle in to watch Marky Mark's funky bunch.

Three episodes in and a few more beers and glasses of wine later, Nick finally gets home and whisks Mel off to bed. I bid them good night and change into some workout pants and a tee I had in my car. I try to fall asleep but I can't. Thinking about Chase has me wound so tight I could snap.

Was he always such an asshole? I never really thought so until today. Well, and when he called off the engagement. I've known him almost my entire life. Living without him is like living without air. I've never known anything different. Every single memory I have includes Chase. We started going out when we were in junior high. Then we broke up freshman year. We both wanted to be free in high school. It lasted just a semester before we got back together. Then we broke up again the summer before our junior year. Chase was feeling a bit too tied down and wanted to play tonsil hockey with a bunch of cheerleaders over the summer.

We got back together senior year, only to break up again when we went to college. It was my turn to sow my oats and get a taste of some college-guy ass. Let's just say I took the opportunity to indulge in a sampler platter of fraternity row. We didn't get back together until we started our teacher credential program. We ended up at the same school and in the same classes, and spent a lot of time catching up on lost time, in bed. The stretch before grad school was our longest time apart. And even though we had split up so many times throughout our lives, we always remained very close friends.

The last time we reunited, we stayed together for ten years. We got engaged after eight of them. Two years after the engagement, we still hadn't set a date for the wedding, and Chase backed out. He moved out of our condo, and five seconds later he was playing house with Summer in some over-priced apartment on the other side of town.

Thinking back now, I can see how ridiculous our relationship was. Ten years, and we never got married. Never even set a date. That should say something. But it doesn't make it any easier. Just thinking about him makes me wish he was here, even with his asshole comments. I hate feeling helpless against his hold over me. Yet, I act like a lovesick child at the mere mention of getting back together. I know deep down it's not going to happen, but just the idea makes me want it more.

And then there's Matty. I don't want him to be the guy that helps me get over Chase. Some guy off the streets could fill those shoes and I wouldn't care. But if, and it's a big if, I were to ever start something, and I don't know what, with him, I'd have to be 100% done with Chase. He deserves that much from me.

So with that in mind, I can't just start hooking up with Matty. He's my dear friend, who just happens to have the most gorgeous eyes, and a messy mane of sandy-blond hair I want to run my fingers through.

Shit. No. I will *not* think of him in such a way. I won't. Move on Shel, but move on without Matty. Without hurting him.

To do list for moving on:

1. ~~Find a rebound guy.~~

1. ~~Find a rebound guy who isn't a teacher.~~

1. Find a rebound guy who isn't a teacher at my school.

Perfect. Melly Belly and I will start looking this weekend.

Chapter Four

The search for the ultimate boyfriend is to be continued. I chickened out, so Mel and I spent the rest of the weekend in our PJs watching Lifetime movies and the Hallmark Channel.

This weekend would've been no different, but I promised my students I'd make it to at least one game this season. Eventually, I will make it out into the big bad world of dating. Maybe.

Tossing my bag on the counter in the restroom, I sift through it for my lip gloss and a brush. The wind tonight has my hair feeling like a rat's nest. You'd think with all the leave-in conditioners and hair polish, my hair would be tame, but no. I always have to curl or straighten it. Or put it up in a clip.

"When was the last time you went to a football game?" I ask Mel.

"Last year some time. Maybe homecoming. Nick and I went with you and Chase, remember?" she responds.

"Yeah, well I don't miss this," I say, brushing the knots out of my brown hair. "Don't get me wrong, I love football something fierce, but high school is just way too slow paced. It's like watching water boil." I stuff my brush back in my bag, and reapply my lip gloss.

Mel finishes washing her hands and then takes out her own tube. Her hair is perfect, and unaffected by the wind. Long, shiny, and straight as a ruler, she lets it hang freely past her shoulders and it wouldn't move even if a tornado touched down on her nose. "Good, so we can cross this shit off our bucket list."

A stall door flings open, and the clack clack of heels echoes through the staff restroom. The reflection in the mirror smirks at me.

"Hey, Summer. I guess Chase is dragging you to these things now," I say with a fake smile, never looking directly at her. "You should really rethink your footwear though. He'll have you on the field moving the chains with him and your heels are gonna get stuck in the ground."

"Forget the chains. Why the hell would you wear stilettos to a game anyway? TMZ isn't following you around with a camera or something, are they?" Mel asks, sarcastically looking around the bathroom.

"Apparently, looking good is only a priority for one of us in here," Summer says, with a click of her tongue.

"You gotta be fucking kidding me, right?" Mel snaps back, turning around to face her.

Summer teases her smooth, long black hair in the mirror, all the while forming the duck lips. "You teach those at-risk kids, don't you, Melissa? You're starting to talk like them. You might want to consider a schedule change," she snickers.

Mel starts taking off her earrings, and she pulls a rubber band off her wrist and twists it in her hair. Then she starts rolling up her sleeves. "Oh, I can do more than just talk like my students. I can act like them too. You want me to show you," she steps forward, throwing up her arms and challenging her.

I want to laugh so hard. This is so Mel, pulling an award-winning Oscar performance. I bet she's snorting inside.

Summer dries her hands, and darts out mumbling, "You guys are fucking crazy."

As soon as she clears the door, Mel and I bust up laughing. Mel has to take a deep breath to calm herself, and her snorting. "Fucking crazy. I'll show her fucking crazy. I'll cut a bitch," she jokes. And then we burst into laughter again. I'm practically convulsing as we exit the bathroom and head toward the bleachers.